**For my pets,
Eevee and Fitzgerald.**

Copyright © 2019 Anne Lambelet

First published in 2019 by Page Street Kids,
an imprint of
Page Street Publishing Co.
27 Congress Street, Suite 105
Salem, MA 01970
www.pagestreetpublishing.com

Distributed by Macmillan, sales in Canada by The Canadian Manda Group

19 20 21 22 23 CCO 5 4 3 2 1

ISBN-13: 978-1-62414-689-3
ISBN-10: 1-62414-689-9

CIP data for this book is available from the Library of Congress.

This book was typeset in Charcuterie.
The illustrations were done in watercolor, pencil, and digital media.
Printed and bound in Shenzhen, Guangdong, China

Page Street Publishing uses only materials from suppliers who are
committed to responsible and sustainable forest management.

Page Street Publishing protects our planet by donating to nonprofits like
The Trustees, which focuses on local land conservation.

DOGS

and their

PEOPLE

Anne Lambelet

PAGE
STREET
KIDS

On beautiful days, when the sun is shining, I like
to take the long way home from school.

And my favorite thing to do is look at all
the dogs and their people.

Some people and their dogs are very young,

and some are very old.

Some dogs and their people look alike,

and others could not be more different.

But no matter what, everyone somehow seems
to have found their perfect match.

Cordelia Vanderlay loves coming to the park to paint,
and Fluffernutter Vanderlay considers herself
a bit of an artist too.

Augustus Pennyfarthing is very little, and
his owner, Sir Archibald Pennyfarthing, is very big,
but everyone knows which one of them
is really in charge.

Jennette and Lisette are twins, but they have very different dogs

to complement their very different styles.

Mr. Pemberton the corgi couldn't find
a better ice-cream buddy than
Little Alexander Wallace,

and I've never seen a better set
of matching mustachios than on
Lord Banberry and his schnauzer, O'Grady.

Mr. Jenkins is tall with a small dog, and
Mrs. Jenkins is small with a tall dog.

They are the perfect couple with
the perfect couple of dogs.

The hot dog vendor, Freddie McDarrow,
has the second-biggest smile in the world, topped only by
the smile of his canine business partner, Ernie.

Watching dogs and their people is fun
because I can always tell they are
best friends.

But no matter how many people
and their dogs I see,

I am always the most excited to get back home
and see *my* best friend, Fitzgerald.

He is my fat, lazy, grumpy old . . .

CAT!